JAWS

BIG SHARK, LITTLE BOAT

A BOOK OF OPPOSITES

By Geof Smith

Illustrated by Kaysi Smith

 A GOLDEN BOOK · NEW YORK

Text copyright © 2023 Universal City Studios LLC. All Rights Reserved. Illustrations copyright © 2023 by Funko, LLC.
Funko, POP!, and trade dress are registered trademarks of Funko, LLC. All Rights Reserved.
Published in the United States by Golden Books, an imprint of Random House Children's Books, a division of Penguin
Random House LLC, 1745 Broadway, New York, NY 10019, and in Canada by Penguin Random House Canada
Limited, Toronto. Golden Books, A Golden Book, A Little Golden Book, the G colophon, and the distinctive gold spine
are registered trademarks of Penguin Random House LLC.

rhcbooks.com

Educators and librarians, for a variety of teaching tools, visit us at RHTeachersLibrarians.com

ISBN 978-0-593-57061-6 (trade) — ISBN 978-0-593-57062-3 (ebook)

Printed in the United States of America

10 9 8 7 6 5 4 3 2 1

Welcome to the little town of Amity Island! People come here to swim, boat, and have fun in the sun. Today there's a special visitor in the water— a very big great white shark!

Everyone is having fun **IN** the water.

But then someone sees a shark fin!

Da-Dum
Da-Dum

Da-Dum

Everyone runs **OUT** of the water. Staying on the beach will be just fine.

Wait! That's a not a shark. It's two kids playing a joke with a **FAKE** fin!

A man in a rowboat sees the **REAL** shark! Row, row, row your boat as quickly as you can. . . .

Police Chief Brody is afraid of the water. He wants to stay **DRY**.

Matt Hooper is a scientist who knows that you have to get **WET** to find sharks. Uh-oh, this shark seems to have very pointy teeth!

Hooper and Brody
head out to sea with
Quint, the fisherman.

Quint climbs **UP** the mast to look for the shark.

Brody stays

DOWN

on the deck.

Suddenly, the shark bursts
out of the water! It is very,
very **BIG**.

The boat suddenly seems very, very **SMALL**.

"You're gonna need a bigger boat," Brody tells Quint.

Hooper leans **OVER** the water and
watches the waves. Where did that shark go?

The shark swims deep **UNDER** the water.

There's the shark! It swims very **FAST**.

The boat chugs after it, but it's too **SLOW**.

Hooper wants a closer look at the big shark. He gets **INSIDE** a cage and goes in the water.

The shark is **OUTSIDE** the cage—and Hooper hopes it stays there!

That night, the shark circles the boat.
It is very **QUIET**.

Chasing sharks is hard work. Quint, Hooper, and Brody stop to rest and sing a **LOUD** song.

Even big sharks get tired.
The shark is ready to head
home. It's time to say goodbye
to Brody, Hooper, Quint, and
Amity Island.

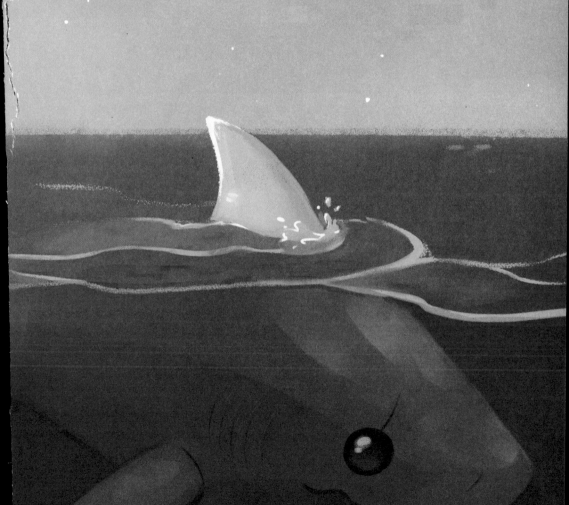

Let's return to the **FRONT** of the book, just in case . . .

. . . the shark comes **BACK!**

Da-Dum